His Blood Cries Out for Justice

W.C. CHANDLER

iUniverse, Inc.
New York   Bloomington

His Blood Cries Out for Justice

iUniverse books may be ordered through booksellers or by contacting:

iUniverse
1663 Liberty Drive
Bloomington, IN 47403
www.iuniverse.com
1-800-Authors (1-800-288-4677)

ISBN: 978-1-4401-8741-4 (pbk)
ISBN: 978-1-4401-8743-8 (cloth)
ISBN: 978-1-4401-8742-1 (ebook)

Printed in the United States of America

iUniverse rev. date: 3/17/10

Contents

1. "Dear Reader" 1

2. "His Blood Cries out" 9

3. "Ollie Chandler" 17

4. Mr. Lane & Ollie 27

5. The Beginning of the End 41

6. Dead Woman Walking..............................53

7. The Family Crisis 59

8. A Brother's Indictment.............................69

9. Postlude 83

CHAPTER 1

"Dear Reader"

Dear Reader,

I am not a writer, nor do I claim to be. This book is written for several reasons, chief among which is my need to somehow purge myself of the negative emotions which have been buried deeply for so long - emotions which have a need to be released, for they have been in control for far too long. I read in the Word of God the following words:

> *"Dearly beloved, avenge not yourselves, but rather give place unto wrath: for it is written, Vengeance is mine; I will repay, saith the Lord."* (Romans 12:19)

I have been a Christian for a number of years, but this scripture did not become a reality in my life until recently. I have, within myself, wanted to see someone pay for what I feel were injustices to my family, especially my brother, Ollie. Even though my brother confessed to a crime that he later swore that he did not commit, he was unfairly and unjustly treated. Through the series of events that happened, an insidious growth began within the deepest recesses of my soul. It has stayed with me for over 40 years – growing and consuming me on a daily basis. Because I was not willing to release it, "it" became my master – consuming my thoughts and sometimes, my actions. I am ready now to face this giant in my life, and to overcome that which has been overcoming. And so, putting pen to paper, my quest for healing begins. This is written from my perspective – as I remember events. It is not an indictment against anyone, per se, but just a catharsis to rid myself of things that have been injurious to me, spiritually and emotionally.

My Remembrances

I suppose, in the whole scheme of things, Ollie Chandler would probably be considered very insignificant. He lived, and he died. He didn't accomplish much – in fact, he never even finished school. He didn't invent anything that would improve the lot of mankind. He didn't marry and raise a family. He didn't make any worthwhile contributions to society. Ollie was a nondescript, 18-year old young man when his life was brutally taken. You might say that if this Ollie was so insignificant by the world's standards, why then would anyone write about him? Who would be interested in reading about a young man whom no one, outside of his family, even remembers?

The answer becomes subjective because, you see, Ollie Chandler was my brother, and he was a significant part of our large family. My mom and dad had 14 children, and Ollie was one of those children. No, he may not have made any important contribution to society; no, he didn't even finish school. He did nothing that anyone would consider worthy of mentioning; but he was my brother. He was the

son of loving parents. He was a creation of God – and that is what makes him important enough to write about.

Can we say that because an individual is considered nondescript by man's standards that he is unimportant? Can we say that because an individual is Black and uneducated that his life has no purpose or meaning? Can we say that because an individual is one of 14 children that he is expendable because, as someone long ago said, " … since his parents have so many other children, this one will not even be missed."

Let me pose a question to you, since the existence or non-existence of Ollie would be considered of little importance to anyone outside of his family. Can you name five persons who, over the past five years, contributed significantly to the field of medicine, or to the field of science, or music, or art? The average person cannot name those who have contributed to the betterment of mankind. It is not the person, but their contribution, which becomes the issue. If people are judged by their contributions to society, why are so many of their names forgotten? Does it matter that

the names be remembered, or is the fact that people exist to fulfill their own destiny the thing that matters most?

I would venture to say that a person's life has meaning to his particular environment. No matter how long or short that life, someone is affected by virtue of the fact that the person lived. He was an integral part of the family into which he was born – because he made that family complete. When one part of a family is removed, there is a void left in that family. This is what happened in the Chandler family. Ollie was a vital part, and when he was gone, there was an emptiness that never was filled.

Our family consisted of daddy, mother and 14 siblings. It was a large family, but each member of the family was crucial to the wholeness and unity of the family. When Ollie died, a void was left, and a part of the unity in our family was destroyed. We were no longer a complete unit, but a fragmented, disjointed, incomplete family which was further torn apart by things which happened before and after Ollie's death.

This account is written to somehow show that Ollie's life had meaning. He was important, if to no one but his family. Ollie lived, he loved, he had feelings, he had purpose, and he had worth. His death, though it happened over 40 years ago, is still keenly felt by those of us who remain. There has not been a day since that tragic time – October 18, 1963, that I have not thought about my brother. I have wondered about the injustice of what happened. I have wondered about what might have been. I have wondered how different my life might have been - for the direction of my life was affected by the death of my brother.

My consciousness has been consumed by memories of Ollie; memories of my mother and father as they struggled to come to grips with the death of their child – but unable to do so, finally ending a 25-year marriage in the divorce court. I have often had dreams of the family as I think how it should have been, with Ollie still a living part, seeing him in his adulthood, with a wife and children – working to see that they had what they needed to sustain life. I sometimes feel like Ebenezer Scrooge in (Dickens's) "A Christmas Carol." Ebenezer was allowed to see the past, present and future through the visitation of three ghosts. I see myself standing on the sidelines of an unfolding drama. I see what could have been, and I weep. I see what should have been, and I mourn. I see what was, and I find myself resisting the anger that tries to overtake me. I resist the urge to go out and make others hurt as my family has been hurt, and are still hurting.

I heard one of my friends say that when he read the history of Black slaves and how they were torn away from their homes and family, and how they suffered and died, he became so angry that he waged war against anyone who was not Black. He knew that people presently had nothing to do with what happened 300 years ago, but the fact that Whites exerted that much control over innocent people caused him to look at the whole race as being the enemy. How I can relate to those feelings! This exercise will be the exorcism that is needed to cleanse my soul – and set me free!

CHAPTER 2

"His Blood Cries out"

"And He said, What hast thou done? The voice of thy brother's blood crieth unto me from the ground." (Genesis 4:10)

The voice of my brother, Ollie's blood is crying out – the same words that were on his lips when his life was brutally snatched away before he had a chance to live. The words "I'm innocent" can still be heard by me and my family. Ollie is crying – "I'm innocent." Just as he cried those same words with his dying breath in 1963, those words are still being cried out today.

In the book of Genesis, the first murder is recorded – an act, which was done in secret, but known to God, the One who knows the very thoughts and intents of the heart. This same God, who already knew the answer, confronted Cain, the murderer with this question (Genesis 4:9):

"Where is Abel, thy brother?"

Cain was given an opportunity to confess to his crime, but not realizing that God already knew what he had done, he asked God a redundant question:

"Am I my brother's keeper?"

And God, grieved not only because of the insensitive, brutal act which had been committed by Cain against his only brother, but also his lack of remorse, said, in Genesis 4:10:

> *"What hast thou done? The voice of thy brother's blood crieth unto me from the ground."*

From the beginning of time, men have committed senseless acts of violence against one another. When the acts are discovered, the perpetrators often shift the blame to innocent persons, thereby excusing themselves in the process. They do not want to be responsible for their acts of violence. Often it is not only the perpetrators who throw suspicion on innocent people, but also the very ones who have been chosen as protectors of society – the very ones who have sworn to uphold the laws of the land, who cast suspicion wrongly.

This is not to say that everyone found guilty of a crime is innocent – No! But when a young man of 17 years of age, in the face of evidence to the contrary, in spite of a "confession," is arrested, beaten, forced to confess to a crime that he did not commit, tried, convicted and executed, this is tantamount to a serious travesty of justice. Even though he confessed to a murder, which he claims he did not commit, this does not excuse those who knew that there were extenuating circumstances, but did nothing to stop an innocent young man from being executed. This does not excuse the law enforcement agents who had knowledge of other people's involvement, but who conveniently hid the evidence, and did not investigate this crucial evidence.

How many people have been jailed and/or executed for crimes, which they did not commit, even when confessions are beaten out of them? This is not an unusual occurrence, as evidenced by the number of innocent individuals who have recently been found innocent (due to DNA evidence) of the crimes that they "supposedly" committed. How much innocent blood is crying out from the ground? How many young people have been sacrificed because they were thought to be expendable? How many have suffered for the sins of others? How many, because of the color of their skin, or other reasons, have been sacrificed on the altar of injustice?

In the December 12, 2005 issue of Time Magazine, the following was stated in an article by Brian Bennett entitled "True Confessions:"

> *"A 2002 study from Northwestern University showed that 59% of all miscarriages of justice in homicide investigations in Illinois*

– where a year later Governor George Ryan commuted all death sentences – involved false confessions. But despite such evidence, few confessions are ever thrown out. According to Richard J. Ofshe, a social psychologist at the University of California, Berkeley, and an expert in false confessions, only recently have juries been allowed to hear testimony about the phenomenon, which can occur as a result of coercion, exhaustion or mental impairment."

The Lord, the righteous judge, is still asking, "Where is your brother?" The very ones who were the executioners are being asked that question. We are all brothers, for we came from a common parentage, regardless of color. A sin against a man by another man is a sin of brother against brother. Those who conducted and participated in courts of injustice and mocking must stand before the final court, whose judge will be the Lord, Himself. They will be tried and convicted as they plead for mercy, and declare their innocence. But just as Ollie cried and declared his innocence until the time of his execution/murder, and a deaf ear was the response to his cries, so will the Judge of the living and the dead turn his ear from their cries for mercy. When justice could have prevailed, or when mercy could have been extended, it was refused. "Guilty! Let him be offered up in the place of another. His life is worthless – therefore, he is expendable."

Little did they know that the shed blood of their distant relative would cry out for forty years to be vindicated! Little did they realize that their blood was and still is inextricably connected to the blood that was shed! When they executed Ollie, they executed a part of themselves. Little did they know that when they called him "guilty" they were condemning themselves!

> "*Be not deceived; God is not mocked: for whatsoever a man soweth, that shall he also reap.*" (Galatians 6:7)

There may be unfairness in the courts of man, but in the final analysis, justice will prevail, for God is the final judge.

He weighs all things and uncovers those things that men, in vain, have tried to hide.

CHAPTER 3

"Ollie Chandler"

Ollie Chandler was a young boy who loved life, and who loved the large family of which he was a part. The family consisted of our mother and father (John and Leatha), and fourteen siblings. We lived in the small rural town of Clyattville, GA, and the times were hard, especially for an African-American family in the '50's. It wasn't easy to find work, and with such a large family, everyone had to do their share in order for the family to survive. Mother and Daddy had a small farm where they were able to raise food to help feed our large family.

The family worked hard for the "White folks" and always received less for their labor than was fair. They were paid whatever the employers decided they wanted to pay. My parents had no other choice than to accept the piddling amounts that they were paid. Life was hard – but for the sake of the family, my parents suffered in silence. Mother always said that it wouldn't always be this way. Times were going to change. But that change was a long time coming, and life remained hard in South Georgia.

As soon as each child was old enough, he or she was sent to the fields to help the family. Depending on the needs of the family, school often had to take a back seat to work. The immediate needs were seen as more important than school. We worked hard in the fields, and were paid sometimes $3.00 a day for our labor. At week's end when we were paid, we took the money and gave it to Mother. This would help to buy shoes, clothing and food for the family. Although we lacked so much in material goods, we had a lot of love for each other. It was not a burden to share, and everyone was willing to help do whatever was necessary for the good of the family. Our love caused the hardships and injustices of those years to be a minor inconvenience. When measured against the affection that we had for each other, our love outweighed everything else. In this family of ten boys and four girls, Mother and Daddy taught us to look out for one another. We were a close-knit family – the older ones always looking out for the younger ones. We survived despite the hardships.

Not only were we taught to love one another, we were taught to love God, and to always put Him first. Despite how we were treated, we were taught to always do the right thing toward everyone. We were taught that God will always make a way, and that one day, things would get better. We were encouraged, that no matter what we did, to always do our best. From early childhood, we were taught good work ethics. Whether we were to get paid or not, work was to be done with a sense of pride. Picking cotton, cropping tobacco, doing chores in our small home, everything that we did was to be done in the best way possible. One of Mother's favorite scriptures was found in Ecclesiastes 9:10:

> *"Whatsoever thy hand findeth to do, do it with thy might ... "*

Our parents instilled a sense of pride in us, and a sense of dignity. Even though the atmosphere was racially charged, we were taught that someday we would have the same opportunities that other people had. We would be able to have good homes, decent jobs and a decent life. Times were hard, and people unfair, but we always tried to hold our heads up and always believed that times were changing. Little did we know that in the midst of our bittersweet existence, our family would be subjected to a tragedy of tantamount proportions. My dear brother, "Ollie" (Oliver) would be falsely accused and convicted of murder, and unjustly executed even while he proclaimed his innocence.

In the south of the '50's, so many African-Americans (we were called "Negroes" then) were killed for something they didn't do. It appeared that it was the "sport" of the white man, and since he had the power and had no fear of retribution, this "sport" was actively pursued. This is not to say that all white people were players, but from my vantage point, it appeared that the majority of whites were either actively or passively playing this game of life to their advantage. This was the environment of the times.

And what were these times like? This was a time of unrest and turmoil. It was a time of the beginning of change – integration was on the horizon. The decade of the'50's and '60's – when the governor of the State of Georgia, Eugene Talmadge, attempted to fight integration by asking the Georgia legislature to withhold funds from any schools which admitted Black students. It was a time when a young Martin Luther King, Jr. was about to graduate from Crozer theological Seminary in Chester, PA. It was a time when Hank Aaron was still playing with the Indianapolis Clowns, a team in the old Negro League. The '50's was also the time when Martin Luther King, Jr. wed Coretta Scott, and Richard B. Russell made a prediction that the Supreme Court would one day vote to end segregation. It was during these years that Ralph McGill predicted that the Supreme Court would declare school segregation unconstitutional, and that Hank Aaron, after playing in the Negro League and excelling in his sport, would be signed by the Milwaukee Braves, breaking the barrier that held Blacks back from major league sports. This was the time when the Supreme Court, in Brown vs. the Board of Education, would hold that racial segregation in public schools was indeed unconstitutional, and the same year that a young Martin Luther King, Jr. would become the pastor of the Dexter Avenue Baptist Church in Montgomery, Alabama.

Hank Aaron continued to make history with his ball playing, helping the National League to win over the American League in 1955; the Supreme Court voted to desegregate public golf courses, playgrounds and beaches as Gov. Talmadge, the governor of "all" the people, declared that the public had the right to "refuse to comply" with what the Supreme Court said; and Rosa Parks refused to move to the back of the bus, and the bus boycott began in Montgomery with Dr. King being thrust into the forefront of the battle. The United States House of Representatives passed the Civil Rights legislation; however, the Senate refused to take up the issue in the election year of 1956 – and the Supreme Court ruled that segregation on city buses was illegal.

The year, 1957, was the year that the Southern Leadership Conference was being founded, with Martin Luther King, Jr. as its leader, and a fight was going on in the Senate with regard to the Civil Rights Bill, which was passed in August 1957 by a vote of 60 to 15. Hank Aaron, although he was continuing his struggle in baseball was named MVP of the National League, while at the same time, Dr. King was stabbed while on a book tour in New York City. Not only were Blacks suffering at the hands of outrageous and ungodly men, but also a Jewish Temple in Atlanta was destroyed – dynamited by the KKK. U.S. District Judge Frank H. Hoople ordered the Atlanta city schools to desegregate, and the sit-ins began in the south as the decade of the '60's began. The University of Georgia admitted Blacks in the midst of a furor as governor Ernest Vandiver attempted to cut off state funding to colleges to prevent Blacks from attending. Charlayne Hunter and Hamilton Holmes were admitted as the first Black students to the University of Georgia, and Gov. Vandiver was charged with the responsibility of "protecting" the very ones he had vowed not to be allowed to enter this prestigious university.

As mid-decade started, we continued to see killings, debates, anger and frustration as the journey to integration continued. Dr. King led a march of 250,000 in Washington, D.C. where he delivered his famous "I Have A Dream" speech. The state of Georgia desegregated every public facility eight months ahead of the time set by the national Civil Rights Act, because the handwriting was on the wall. The thrust by the white establishment was being toppled; the dams had broken, and the rush of the waters of fairness and equity were plunging and threatening to flood anyone who tried to stop them. It was in this environment of hostility and anger at the government that my brother, Ollie, found himself enmeshed.

This was the environment of the decades of the '50's and '60's of which we were products. Although the courts had legislated integration, it could not legislate a person's heart; and segregation and unfair treatment were alive and well in South Georgia. We saw the closing of Black schools and the opening of private "Christian" schools – so that white children would not be subjected to the "shame" of going to school with Black children. These were the times in South Georgia.

Chapter 4

Mr. Lane & Ollie

Mr. Hugh Vaughn Lane, Jr. was a wealthy 49-year old farmer who lived alone on his 300-acre farm in a little place outside of Valdosta called Clyattville, in Lowndes County, GA. Mr. Lane was a divorcee, and resided in his six-room house, which was located on his property. Mr. Lane had worked as a trucking firm operator, and it was said that he held stocks in several major business concerns. According to newspaper accounts, Mr. Lane's wealth was estimated to be as much as $100,000, but he lived in a shabby 6-room house and kept all the doors, except for the back door, nailed shut. It was this Mr. Lane who hired Ollie to work on his farm.

Ollie came running home excitedly. "Mother – Daddy," he called as he bounded in the door. "Mr. Lane wants me to work for him. He said that I'm a good worker – one of the best he has ever seen, and he offered me a job." Ollie was so happy and pleased that he would be working steadily. It would be a big help to the family to have someone else with a steady paycheck. My parents were grateful to Mr. Lane for giving little Ollie the opportunity to work for him.

Ollie was a strong boy, although he was mentally challenged. The family never let this be a factor, and it never occurred to us that Ollie was "slow" until it was determined by the courts prior to his trial that Ollie had some mental challenges. Ollie only went to the 6th grade, and was never a good student. He was polite and mannerable, but he had a very low IQ. After 6th grade, Ollie decided to go to work to help out, since he was one of the "older" children. In the south of the '50's and '60's, many young people, especially Blacks, quit school in order to work and help to support their families. Ollie worked in Hastings, Florida (just outside St. Augustine) as a seasonal worker for a while. He would go on a bus with other seasonal workers, and work for the week on the farms in Hastings and come home on the weekends. It was during one of the off seasons that Mr. Lane approached Ollie about working for him. This meant, to Ollie, that he would be working fulltime. He would work during the harvesting season in Hastings, and during the off-seasons and weekends that he was home for Mr. Lane. It was a perfect set-up for Ollie, and it provided him with money to not only help the family, but to use for himself. Ollie was so pleased to be able to help to support his brothers and sisters.

After Ollie had been working for Mr. Lane for about seven months, Mr. Lane visited the house to meet my parents and the rest of the family. Mr. Lane seemed to be a decent man, and seemed to genuinely care for our family. He would come over often and sit on the porch talking to Mother and Daddy. He talked about what a good worker Ollie was, and how impressed he was with the good work ethics that he exhibited. Ollie worked for Mr. Lane for several years, and because Mr. Lane was a fair-minded person and paid a fair wage, other people in the community didn't like him. The fact that he came to our house to visit was not acceptable to some people. The times seemed to dictate that if one was white and in the south, there should be a natural hatred for Blacks. This was true where we lived, and because Mr. Lane didn't fit the mold, his white "brothers" hated him as much as they hated Blacks. Mr. Lane was termed a "nigger-lover" and this was an anathema to the white culture.

Mr. Lane became a good friend of the family. He loved Ollie and told my parents that he was happy to have Ollie as his employee, but especially as his friend. Mr. Lane was aware of the hatred that was directed at him by his peers, and even mentioned to some of his friends that he was afraid of "someone." He told them that if anything ever happened to him, to call the police. He didn't mention names, but it was apparent to those with whom he spoke that he was fearful of someone. Newspaper reports stated the following, which was reported by Mr. Lane's close friend, Ben Bates:

"Bates said Lane had told him to come looking for him if he should be missed for several days."

Why would Mr. Lane make that request? And, if he was afraid of someone hurting him, why continue to keep Ollie on as his employee? Who was Mr. Lane fearful of?

One day, according to accounts, Mr. Lane went to the bank and withdrew a large sum of money. According to newspaper reports, however (Valdosta Daily Times, 1962), Mr. Lane did not go to the bank to withdraw money, but to deposit a large sum. Neighbors and friends reported that Mr. Lane never carried much money on his person – only a few dollars. The news story reported that, " …several neighbors and friends reported Lane had shown them a deposit slip for $7,200 on Monday. Talk about the deposit could have become twisted, it is speculated, and the murderer could have been led to believe that Lane had a sizable amount of money in his home."

Whatever the truth is, the report is that Mr. Lane went to the bank and made a large withdrawal, and hid the money somewhere in the house. Ollie had just finished working for the day, and was preparing to start home. Ollie would have had no knowledge of any bank transactions, and would have had no knowledge of what had transpired. At this time, Ollie had been working for Mr. Lane for some time, and was a trusted employee. Ollie had keys to Mr. Lane's barn, and was allowed to use the tools and other items in the barn as he needed. When Ollie finished his chores for the day, he went to Mr. Lane's house to let him know that he was finished for the day. According to Ollie, he found Mr. Lane dead on the floor, shot to death, and he also discovered that some men were still in the house. These men, knowing that Ollie worked for Mr. Lane, knew how easy it would be to frame a "nigger" for the murder – and this is what I believe they set out to do. Who would take the word of a "nigger" against that of decent white men!!! And so, the saga began.

The person or persons who killed Mr. Lane knew of his affection for my family, and as a result, did not like Mr. Lane. Ollie was only seventeen years old when he was arrested for Mr. Lane's murder. According to one of Mr. Lane's relatives, the police questioned a man who they found with blood on his shirt, but he was released. Witnesses also said that a couple was seen leaving Mr. Lane's house around 10:00 am on the morning of his murder. They were driving a 1948 or 1949 Chevrolet. This couple was never sought nor questioned in connection with the murder. The man with blood on his shirt was released, and my brother was arrested. The money – if there was any, was never recovered, and no money was ever found on my brother.

My young, innocent, naïve brother was arrested, constantly proclaiming his innocence of the events which had happened. He was arrested in Hastings, FL (near St. Augustine where he worked). He was returned to Valdosta where he was arraigned. It was in Lowndes County where he was starved and beaten unmercilessly until he confessed to a crime that I (as well as others who were living in the area) don't believe he committed. One of the Black inmates who was incarcerated during this time, told my parents that he saw Ollie after the beating. Ollie was beaten so badly that he was bruised and swollen about the head and face. My father and mother saw Ollie some days after the beating, and they were horrified at what they saw. When my father told the rest of the family about Ollie's condition, he wept bitterly. This is the first time that I ever remember seeing my dad shed tears.

When Ollie surprised the person or persons in the house immediately after Mr. Lane's murder, he was forced to put his hand on the gun (which was recovered at Mr. Lane's house) and on Mr. Lane's wallet so that his fingerprints would be on both. (This was according to what Ollie told my dad.) He was illegally arrested, charged and convicted by an all-white jury. My brother died as a result of an unjust, racist system.

The family could not afford to hire a lawyer, so the Lowndes County Court appointed one for him. The lawyer, who was 82 years old at the time, stated at the hearing that he was "too tired" to argue the case. He needed some time to prepare himself adequately, and the case was set for a later date. Of course, this worked in the prosecution's favor because Ollie had only a few months until his 18th birthday at which time he would legally be an adult and could be tried as such.

The attorney was not granted a hearing to present evidence in the case. It seems as though Ollie had been found guilty of this crime long before the trial began. Everyone who knew Ollie knew that he was innocent of this heinous crime. He had worked for Mr. Lane as a trusted employee for several years, and always respected him. There was so much evidence that was not allowed to be entered into the record. The shells, which were found, didn't match the gun, which authorities said was used to kill Mr. Lane. The timeline of the events proved that Ollie was not even near the house when Mr. Lane was attacked. The money (if there was money involved) was never found – and even though Ollie was beaten so severely, he could never relate to them what happened to the money. It was also proven by the court that Ollie was borderline mentally retarded. There was evidence of a low IQ, and according to his teachers Ollie had a difficult time learning in school. The pattern of action, which the prosecutor claimed had happened, was indicative of someone of greater intelligence than Ollie possessed. The defense attorney strongly contended that Ollie should be acquitted on the grounds that he did not have the mental capacity to plan the crime. Even if he had committed the crime, the attorney argued that he was not responsible for his act because his mentality was such that, according to the law, he could not be held criminally responsible. Not only that, Ollie was a minor. In either case, he should have been found "not guilty."

Notice on the next few pages partial copies of letters, which Ollie sent to the family during his incarceration, and determine within yourself whether he had the mental capacity to plan and carry out the murder of Mr. Lane. The letters are not dated, but from the writing, it can be determined that they were written while Ollie was being held. The letters have been untouched, and are copied just as Ollie wrote them. Two of the letters are to my father, and the other to my cousin. The letters were found in my mother's purse after a fire in the home. They had been sent to her after Ollie's death, as well as some other personal effects. Mother kept the letters with her – and her purse was the only thing that escaped the wrath of the fire that destroyed the home.

DEAR FATHER,

HOW ARE YOU. I AM DING
PRETTY GOOD. I DECIDE TWO
RIGHT YOU A FEW LINES TWO LET
YOU HEAR FROM ME. DADDY. I
AM STILL PRAYING AND READING
MY BIBLE. AND TRUSPING IN THE
LORD; DADDY I WANT TWO SEE
YOU, I AM GOING TWO TELK THE
TRUTH. DADDY I DONT WANT
TWO TELK THE TRUTH TWO NO
BODY BUT YOU ARE MR MCCALL.
I DONT HAVE ENEM BUSINESS
IN HEAR, DAY NO I DIDNT
THAT. DADDY I NO WHO WAS THA
MAN WHET MADE ME DO THAT.
DADDY I WANT YOU TWO ALSC
I WANT YOU TWO GO. TWO
ADEL, GA. AND TELK MR MCCALL.
THIS AND MAKE SURE YOU DO
THIS. FOR ME. I AM HEAR IN
THIS JAIL HOUSE. I NO I DON
HAVE ENEM BUSNESS IN THIS
JAIL HOUSE I WANT YOU ALL
TWO COME AND GET ME OUT O
THIS O JAIL HOUSE. ¢ — OVER—

ST. AUGUSTINE, OTHER
WOULD OF
READY
                WOULDNT HAVE
THAT THESE PEOPLES TWO
LET ME OUT OF HEAR. DADDY, I
WANT YOU TWO BREING ME SOME
FRUIT WHEN YOU COME SUNRAY.
TELK MOTHER THAT I SAY
HELLO. AND ALSO THE CHILDREN.
SO DADDY, I AM STILL PRAYING.
AND YOU ALL KET PRAING FOR
ME ME. TWO. GRACE BE WANT
YOU ALL AND ALSO GRACE BE WITH
ME. FROM GOD. AND THE LORD
JESUS CARIST. THE LORD LOVE
ME. AND THE LORD LOVE YOU A
TWO. SO I WILL CLOSE MY
LOVEETH LETTER. MAKE GOD BLES
YOU ALL. AND KET YOU ALL. SO
THIS WILL BE AIL FOR THIS
TIME

        TRUELY YOUR FROM
        OLIE CHANDLER
        TWO FATHER.
        MAKE GOD BLESS YOU All
        A. MAN.

HELLO MAR.

HOW ARE YOU. FINE I HOPE
I BESIDE TWO RIGHT YOU
A FREE LAWT TWO LET YOU
HEAR FROM ME TWO DAY. O. K.
TELK ALL HELLO MY LOVE IS TRUE.
HEAR MY PRAYNG. O O GOD. MAR I
AM STILL PRAYING AND TRUSTETH
IN GOD. THE BLAY THAT I CAN.
AND YOU ALL KET PRAKING FOR
ME. BY THE WAY MAR LET ME
HEAR FROM YOU. O. K. IT BEAT
A LOND TIME SENTOYW. I HEAC
FROM YOU. LET ME HEAR FROM
YOU BABBY. O. K. YOU AM
SAYKETH FOR GOT ME ARE YOU.
BY OTHE WAY LET ME HEAR
FROM YOU. O. K. MAR. YOU DID
TELK ME OTHE TRUTH YOU DID
COME TWO SEE ME. SAY COMP
YOU ANES LIE THAT. TELK ME
THE TRUTH. O. K. HOW RANK
THAT. SO MAR I WILL CLOSE
MY LETTER. MAKE GOD BLESS YOU
ALL AND KET YOU. LONEY OLIE
TRUEK YOUR. FROM
OLIE TWO MAR. O. K.

CHAPTER 5

The Beginning of the End

Ollie was arrested in 1962. According to news reports, Ollie was arrested in Hastings, FL where he was working seasonal work. For a whole year, he was taken back and forth between Valdosta and St. Augustine, Florida – for no apparent reason. He was seventeen when he was arrested, and the trial began in 1963 when he had just turned eighteen. The trial was just a formality because they already knew what they were going to do. Ollie had already been tried and found guilty before the trial started. The authorities had beaten a confession out of him shortly after his arrest. According to newspaper accounts, Ollie was arrested at a "Negro labor camp" in Hastings, Florida where he had allegedly fled after the murder. If he was on the run, why would he return to the place where he was working – and where he knew that authorities would look for him? After his arrest, he was taken to the county jail in St. Augustine, Florida, where authorities claim that he waived extradition and agreed to return to Lowndes County. He was returned to Valdosta, GA by authorities that claimed that Ollie gave the following statement:

> *"Wednesday about noon Hugh V. Lane, Jr. and me had an argument about wages. He was paying me $5 a day and owed me for a day and a half. He said he wasn't going to pay me and kicked at me. He left and said he was going to a phone."*

> *"While he was gone, I went into the house, got his shotgun, a 12-gauge single barrel, and when he came back I was standing in the living room and I shot him."*

> *"I took his pocketbook, took $60 out of it and threw the pocketbook in the woodpile.*

After I shot him I put him in the closet and left the farm. I caught a ride into Valdosta and caught the bus about 2 o'clock and came to Hasting."

According to reports, Mr. Lane was killed on Tuesday morning. The "confession" states the crime happened on Wednesday. The explanation by authorities for this discrepancy was that "the teen-age Negro was mixed up about the day on which the crime was committed." Was Ollie also mixed up about the day he took the bus and supposedly returned to Hastings - if, in fact, he did? And if Mr. Lane was so angry with Ollie, he certainly would not have left his house and left the door unlocked. How did Ollie get into the house in order to wait for Mr. Lane? And, according to friends who said that Mr. Lane never carried more than a $2 or $3 dollars on his person, how could Ollie have taken $60, as the "confession" has stated? And if, according to newspaper reports, Mr. Lane's shotgun was in need of repair, how did Ollie shoot him with that gun? Notice the report:

> " ...*reported Lane's shotgun was an old-model Remington given to him by his father. Lane had attempted to get the gun repaired, but the factory reported that parts for it were out of date.*"

Another discrepancy is that authorities said that when Ollie was arrested, he still had on the shoes that he wore during the time of the slaying, but he "washed the blood off of them." Why did they not check the shoes for traces of blood? Blood cannot be simply "washed off" – there would have been traces of blood left. Another claim by authorities in one newspaper account was that as Ollie was being returned to Valdosta, he said that he could show them where he threw Lane's billfold, but "the trio was unable to find it as they stopped at the farm enroute to the Lowndes County jail." However, in another account, it was stated that Mr. Lane's billfold and keys were stolen, but in the confession, only the billfold was mentioned. Authorities claim that the billfold was found in the bottom of a dry well, and the car keys were discovered in a woodpile near Mr. Lane's home.

There are many discrepancies in Ollie's testimony that did not agree with the evidence that was reported by authorities. This is not an attempt to try the case, for I am not a legal expert. I just notice, in reading the newspaper accounts and looking at Ollie's confession, that there are some inconsistencies. Evidently, these issues were not brought up in court; however, I was not a part of the court proceedings. I am just writing about the events from my own remembrances and from newspaper accounts, which were written during this time.

Also, authorities claim that Ollie said "he placed the shotgun in a corner in the front bedroom because that was where he got it." However, according to the newspaper reports:

"Neighbors said it was well-known that Lane kept the loaded shotgun on a rack by the back door and that he took the weapon into his front bedroom each night."

If this is so, why did Ollie not put the gun back on the rack by the back door if Mr. Lane kept it there during the day? And if bloody clothes were stashed "under a dresser in a home in Hastings, FL, why would Ollie have taken or worn bloody clothes back to his job in Florida? And if, according to reports, other "personal items" were taken from Mr. Lane's house, what happened to the other items? Ollie's confession only mentioned the billfold – not keys or other items. Prior to his "confession," the newspaper reports said, "Mr. Lane's billfold and **other personal effects** were missing from the body." After his arrest, however, reports then stated only money and keys as being the stolen items. No other "personal effects" were mentioned.

For a whole year, after his arrest in 1962, Ollie was taken back and forth between Valdosta and St. Augustine, Florida for no apparent reason. He was seventeen when he was arrested, and the trial began when he had just turned eighteen. I feel that the trial was just a formality because the authorities already knew what they were going to do. Ollie had already been tried and found guilty. According to Ollie, the authorities had beaten him upon his arrest and prior to his confession. Another strange occurrence, which happened while Ollie was awaiting trial, is that the authorities took him to a white Baptist church where he was baptized. My family and I thought that this was strange and we have never had an explanation of why this was done. Our family had always belonged to Payton A.M.E. Church, and Ollie had been a member there all of his life. We have often wondered why the sheriff thought it necessary to have Ollie baptized in a white church.

As stated, the trial was held in 1963, with Ollie being tried by an all-white jury, which consisted of both male and female jurists. In that day, of course, Blacks were not allowed to sit on a jury – and had they been able to do so, I'm sure that the prosecution would have challenged each Black who might have been qualified to sit, and preempted their participation. Ollie was charged with first-degree murder, for the authorities claimed the following:

> **"Judging from the evidence, Futch said it appears that the slaying was premeditated and Chandler will be charged with first-**

> *degree murder, which can mean the death*
> *penalty upon conviction. "*

During the so-called trial, no witnesses were called, and when Ollie's court-appointed attorney tried to call witnesses, he was denied. He was not allowed to present the contradictory evidence which he had and which would have cast suspicion on Ollie's guilt. The judge did not allow the jury to hear information about Ollie's mental challenges, nor any other information other than what the prosecutor presented. Ollie never stood a chance, and he was convicted and sentenced to die in the electric chair.

After the sentencing, I would hear my Mother praying late at night - "Lord, please don't let them take my child away." Mother knew in her heart that Ollie was not guilty, and to hear her crying like that would make me sad for her, but angry at the system. I would cry with her as I listened to her pour her heart out. Why was this happening? What had Ollie done to be treated this way? I have learned over the years that some things have no logical or reasonable explanation. Ollie was sacrificed in the place of Mr. Lane's real killer or killers.

Ollie was found guilty of the crime of first-degree murder, and was sentenced to die in the electric chair. To be found guilty of first-degree murder, premeditation must be established. If, according to the original accounts, robbery was the motive, and since Ollie had no knowledge of Mr. Lane's intent to withdraw money out of the bank and hide it in the house, how could he have planned this crime? Since Ollie had worked for Mr. Lane for such a long time, what was his motive for killing Mr. Lane? What was he going to use the money for? Where was the money that was supposed to have been the motive for his crime? Where was the intent? How did he get into the house without breaking in? How could he have shot Mr. Lane when he was, at the time of the murder, out in the field working? Without any of these questions even being considered, my brother was found guilty of this heinous crime. There is an automatic appeal procedure in place for capital murder convictions, but Ollie's attorney was not allowed to appeal the verdict – and after just a few months, Ollie was transported to the place where he would be put to death.

Still proclaiming his innocence, Ollie was taken to Reidsville, GA by the Lowndes county sheriff. Strangely, following the sheriff's car was a hearse that was to be used to transport Ollie's remains back to Valdosta after the execution. I always thought that it was strange. Ollie was put to death for the murder of Mr. Lane at the young age of 18. My father and an uncle went to the prison in Reidsville to witness the execution, and my father was never the same afterwards. Why? Not only was my father's innocent son being put to death, but in such a cruel manner. Perhaps a brief description of what happens to the prisoner during an execution will help you to understand the enormity of the situation. For a guilty man to be put to death might be understandable and might be deserved; but for an innocent man, who was railroaded into confessing to a crime which he did not commit, to be killed in this way is a travesty of justice:

> *"According to Judge Brennan, the prisoner's eyeballs sometimes pop out and rest on his cheeks. The prisoner often defecates, urinates, and vomits blood and drool. The*

body turns bright red as its temperature rises, and the prisoner's flesh swells and his skin stretches to the point of breaking. Sometimes the prisoner catches on fire, particularly if he perspires excessively. Witnesses hear a loud and sustained sound like bacon frying, and the sickly smell of burning flesh permeates the chamber. There is some debate about what the electrocuted prisoner experiences before he dies, many doctors believe that he feels himself being burned to death and suffocating, since the shock causes respiratory paralysis as well as cardiac arrest. According to Harold Hillman, 'It must feel very similar to the medieval trial by ordeal of being dropped in boiling oil.' Because the energy of the shock paralyzes the prisoner's muscles, he cannot cry out." 'My mouth tasted like cold peanut butter. I felt a burning in my head and my left leg, and I jumped against the straps,' according to Willie Francis, a 17-year old

> **who survived his execution in 1946. Francis**
> **was successfully executed a year later."**

As an aside, it is interesting to note that from 1924 until 1964, there were 417 electrocutions in the state of Georgia – and my brother was one of these.

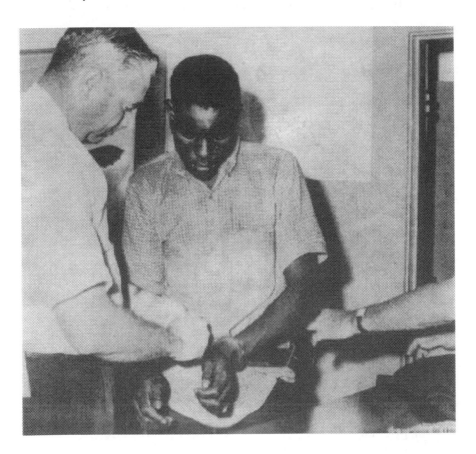

CHAPTER 6

Dead Woman Walking

If you have ever seen a "dead person walking," then you have seen my mother. My mother, who had been so alive and vibrant prior to Ollie's arrest, conviction and execution, became a shell of her former self. Mother was so strong and she and my Dad reared us with a gentle, yet firm hand. Anytime there are fourteen children in a family, there has to be discipline and order. My mother was a strict disciplinarian and she saw to it that her children knew their place. There was a job for each of us to do. The older children went to work in the fields, and the younger ones had their chores in the home. Though there was a lot of work to do, there was an abundance of love. But after Ollie's arrest, Mother began her decline. Though she still held out hope that Ollie would be acquitted, it was a remote hope. When a young Black man was arrested during these times, conviction usually followed – whether guilty or not. There seemed to be a foregone conclusion that all Blacks who were arrested were guilty of the crime for which they had been arrested. During the long months prior to Ollie's trial, conviction and ultimate execution, Mother prayed constantly. She believed that prayer held the key to rectifying this miscarriage of justice.

During these months, Mother felt so helpless because there was nothing that she could do to help her son.   There was no way that she could prove that he was innocent. All Mother could do was to pray. I can still hear her praying – "Lord, help my son. My son is in trouble – Lord, please help my son. I can't do nothing to help him, Lord – no one will listen to him but you, Lord – so Lord, please help my son."

Mother and Daddy would lie awake at night just praying and trying to figure out a way to help Ollie. They were disturbed at the way that he was being treated, and how the authorities were treating the family. Had it not been for the "informant" within the jail, we would have had no word about Ollie at all. The authorities didn't seem to think that we deserved to know Ollie's condition or anything about him at all. We were all helpless – and Mother would say to us that she prayed that no other mother would have to go through what she was going through. She and Daddy felt like failures as parents because there was nothing they could do to help their beloved son. When Mother understood that Ollie was most likely going to die, despite her prayers, her very soul died within her.

I can still see my dear Mother on her bed with two of her sisters lying on either side of her. The day of the execution had approached, and my aunts were attempting to comfort Mother as we all waited for the phone call saying that Ollie had either been executed, or by some miracle, had his sentence commuted. Of course, the phone call came that he had been executed. My Mother and the family were never the same after this happened. My Mother cried so many tears, and she became utterly helpless when she realized that her son had been executed. She had prayed for so long, hoping against hope that her child would be spared and be given a life sentence. At least, (I supposed) she reasoned within herself, she would be able to see him and to talk to him. Even if the guilty person was never brought to justice, she would settle to see her son spend the rest of his life in prison. That would be a small price to pay for the joy of at least having her son alive. But this was not to be.

She never talked much after Ollie was executed and I often wonder just what her thoughts were. Mother would just sit and cry, never really alive. O yes, she was breathing and functioning – but just barely. She was like a robot, doing those things that she had to do in order for the family to survive. She was like a person who was alive, but not alive; dead, but not dead. Her eyes were vacant as she stared off in the distance, not really seeing at all. She existed in her own world – enclosed within herself – not able to share her thoughts with anyone. It was as if she crawled into a hole and pulled it in after her. She ceased to be who she had been. She was never able to come back to reality after she lost her son. But, as the people had said, she still had thirteen other children. She would never miss one!!!

Parents – especially mothers – will do anything for their children. When a Mother faces a situation, which does not allow her to help her child, it is devastating for her. For a mother to see her child pay for a crime, which he committed, is a terrible ordeal; but to see her child pay for a crime that she believes he did not commit is heartrending. Death is final – and even if there had been an investigation in later years and Ollie was found not to be guilty, there would have been no consolation for my Mother. Yes, we might prove that Ollie was not guilty of the murder of Mr. Lane, but to what end? Is the knowledge of knowing that someone else committed the murder consolation enough? Will the years somehow roll back and allow our family to become a family again? Will this knowledge end the devastation, which my family suffered as a result of what we believe to be a miscarriage of justice?

CHAPTER 7

The Family Crisis

This was an extremely difficult time, and our parents tried to keep things together as best they could. It was a very stressful time, and my mother was so heartbroken that she was almost unable to function. On the day of the execution, she was lying in bed, weeping her heart out for her child. Someone very cruelly said that Mother and Daddy had so many children that they wouldn't miss Ollie. Two of Mother's sisters tried to comfort her, but she was so distressed that her child was being murdered for something that he didn't do. She was beyond any earthly comfort — and kept crying out to Jesus for her child.

Mother and Daddy were married for more than twenty-five years, but with the strain of the events, which happened, they were unable to come to grips with working to keep the marriage together. They were just filled with guilt, thinking that there should have been something that they could have done for Ollie. Daddy left about four years after Ollie's death – but to his credit, I will say that he stayed until after most of the children were grown or in their teens. Daddy divorced Mother and moved to the small town of Quitman, which is very close to Valdosta, where he remarried. Even though he and Mother were no longer together, the children kept in touch with both parents. We never knew why our parents divorced, but we knew that we still loved them, regardless of issues that they were unable to resolve among themselves. Mother had a heart attack, and died in 1985, and Daddy passed away in 1996. After Ollie died, Mother was heartbroken; and for the next twenty years, she was unable to bounce back from this devastating time. She tried, for the sake of the family, to be as normal as possible, but it was difficult for her because she was always thinking about Ollie and the injustices that had been perpetrated against him.

Our parents died praying that one day the record would be set straight, and that Ollie would be exonerated for the crime for which he had been executed. Three of the other siblings, Larry, Betty and Mannie C. also died with the same prayer. We know that Ollie is innocent, and that he was used as a scapegoat. Not too long ago we were told by someone that during a bible study, a white minister spoke of an event that he had witnessed while he was a child. The event happened four decades ago and he said that he saw Ollie Chandler's remains being taken to the funeral home by the mortician. The minister said the following:

> "I wouldn't ever again want to see an act of such inhumane magnitude perpetrated against any human being. He was so badly burned – and for a crime he didn't commit."

It also came to our attention that a certain man was in the hospital on his deathbed proclaiming, "they killed that nigger (Ollie) for nothing. He didn't kill Mr. Lane." We found out that this man was Mr. Lane's son-in-law. He knew that Ollie was innocent, and knew that there were others involved in the crime; however, he did not name these persons before his death. He talked about the man who had blood on his shirt, but after the authorities questioned him about this, they did not pursue these leads. They were determined that a "nigger" would die for the murder of Mr. Lane – and Ollie just happened to be convenient.

Just as this minister and others knew forty years ago that Ollie was innocent, our family has known it all along. There is someone out there who is still alive who knows the truth of what happened. Ollie wrote several letters to my father, that were never seen until long after Ollie had been executed. Ollie proclaimed his innocence in these letters, but they did not come to my father until long after Ollie had been executed. Ollie's letters are seen on previous pages, just as he wrote them – misspelled words still intact. As you read them, you can feel the fear and the hurt and the desperation in Ollie. The question remains – "Who killed Mr. Lane?" On the day that Ollie was to go to the electric chair, the family stood around the phone praying and hoping that the phone would ring and that we would hear a voice on the other end saying that Ollie had been pardoned. We knew that it was wishful thinking, but we remained hopeful until the very end.

Although my parents were divorced four years after Ollie's death, our family remained strong, and those of us who are left are still strong. The telling of this story has been heartbreaking for me, but I feel that it is necessary to tell the truth of what happened to my brother. The event happened over forty years ago, but as we all think about those days, the hurt is still there. I wonder if the person or persons who committed this crime have any feelings of those days so long ago. I wonder if they think about the fact that Ollie was executed for a crime that he/she/they committed. I wonder how they can live with themselves knowing that they took two innocent lives – Mr. Lane's and Ollie's. I wonder if they realize that they caused heartache to two innocent families – and caused so much hurt that has remained over the years. I wonder about the value system of the persons who stood around and let this injustice happen. I wonder about the justice system that allowed such discrepancies and unlawful things to happen. I wonder about my mother and father, and think that their twenty-five years should not have ended in divorce. I wonder about my mother, who died of a broken heart – grieving until the very end of her life about her son, Ollie. I wonder what all of our lives would have been had this event in 1963 not happened. I wonder about Ollie and his life – what kind of man he would be at the age of sixty – which is the age he would be now. Would he have gotten married and had children? Would he still be living here in the south? Would all of our lives be any different than they are now? These are questions that will never be answered – because the times dictate otherwise. We cannot go back in time and recapture anything that has been missed or that has been stolen from us. We must live with the pain, hurt, injustices, the lies, the hypocrisy, the inhumane treatment of one human being by another just because of the color of one's skin. How far have we come since 1963?

The writing of the events, from my recollection, has been a catharsis for me. There has been so much – pent-up anxiety and unshed tears over the years, and the penning of this story has allowed some measure of healing – although no resolution. Although we may never know the truth in this life of what happened so many years ago, I am comforted by the scripture in Luke 12:2-3:

> "For there is nothing covered, that shall not be revealed; neither hid, that shall not be known."

> "Therefore whatsoever ye have spoken in darkness shall be heard in the light; and that which ye have spoken in the ear in closets shall be proclaimed upon the housetops."

If we never find out in this life, we can be assured that God knows the full account of the events that took place so many years ago – and we take comfort in that.

I liken my brother to the poor beggar in St. Luke 16:19 who, in innocence, sat by the rich man's gate, begging for crumbs. He didn't want much – only to be given what others didn't want. Ollie was such an innocent. He didn't ask for much, just the chance to do what he could, and receive some compensation for his work. He wanted to be treated as a human, which is the right of birth. Instead, just as the poor beggar, Ollie was treated more cruelly than an animal, and stepped over and stepped on. The beggar found peace in Abraham's bosom. I am certain that my innocent, trusting brother has found joy and comfort in the bosom of Abraham. I pray that my brother, who suffered unspeakable horror in this life at the hands of cruel and unreasonable men. Has been allowed to find that same measure of peace.

"His Blood Cries Out."

As I continue to reflect on this painful and shameful memory of my brother, other memories flood my soul. I think about my teachers in high school and how they would look down on me as if I was guilty of the crime of which my brother had been executed. My sister and I were ridiculed and scorned. We were treated as if we were nobody. I particularly remember one teacher who upset my sister and me so much that we did the only thing that we could do – we began to "act out" in the classroom. She had done so much finger pointing at us that we were simply tired of her accusations and nasty treatment. My sister and I were so upset that we just couldn't calm down. After this had gone on for some time, the teacher finally realized that she was wrong to accuse us. She acknowledged that her job was to teach and not to point accusing fingers at her students.

Other memories of these times continue to stand out in my memory, and have caused some consternation in my life. Several times I have been called to serve jury duty, but because of this incident with my brother, I respectfully declined to serve. When I explained to the presiding judge my reason for not wanting to serve on a jury – especially criminal cases, he would immediately excuse me. He understood my reluctance to serve, and realized that I would be biased. He knew that I could not be impartial and honest in my judgment of those who stood accused of crimes – especially if they were Black.

I think that it will be different now that I have had a chance to put pen to paper and write out my lingering thoughts. I have been able to face the shadows of yesterday, and look forward to what will be in the future. No, I cannot change any thing that has happened, but I can look within and release those demons that have oppressed me for so long.

My energy in this area has been expended – and I look for positive ways to let my life reflect what can yet be.

CHAPTER 8

A Brother's Indictment

This is to the judges and to the prosecutor and all those who were involved, including the witnesses to the charge against my brother, Oliver, who was framed for Mr. Lane's murder; and to the jury and witnesses who knew in their heart and soul the my brother was framed. At the end I do believe the judge, jury, and witnesses will stand before God when the book is opened and when the charge is read. This is when my brother will get justice. But I guess until then my brothers, sisters and myself will cry out for justice. Our brother's blood will cry out from the grave for justice. But to those of you who were involved in this case, and knew that a young boy of seventeen was being held in the

Lowndes County Jail for one year until he reached the age of eighteen, and his life was then abruptly taken away for a crime he did not commit; and all of you who knew he was not guilty, and to the all white jury, prosecutor and judge, know that you were all wrong for the way my brother, Oliver was killed in the electric chair. Furthermore, he was not just electrocuted; he was burned almost to a crisp until some parts of his body would crumble just like dry wood.

But the Bible says that our sin would testify against us. And Oh yes, you that were involved in murdering and the killing of my brother, you won't have to say one word. When the book is opened and the question is asked, "Did you kill Oliver Chandler?" You won't have to say a word. Your sin will testify against you, like you were a witness for the prosecution. My Bible tells me that your sin will testify against you. The only thing about that is you will have more than one murder against you. You see you will be charged with killing our mother, too because her heart could not take any more suffering. Oh, I still cry now about my sixteen year old brother that was taken away from the whole family and me. We used to get together and sing and play ball and just have fun together.

I can imagine he ran so hard when they forced him to get out of town. If he hadn't, they would have killed him. They also made threats to the family and all he could think about was finding Daddy, so he could help him. And after he told his Dad what happened, including the threats they had made to the family, I can imagine that our Dad was confused and afraid for his son's life, as well as the entire family's life, thinking and wondering what he could do or say to keep his family safe. After all Ollie did leave town to go back to his seasonal job before it was time because he was so afraid after the Lowndes County Sheriff's Department and G.B.I. was so sure that it was Ollie who killed Mr. Lane. But oh how wrong they all were. Another reason they were sure they had the right person is because Ollie was working for Mr. Lane. They went down to Florida and arrested Ollie for a crime he did not commit.

Oh I remember how he pleaded for his life saying that he was innocent. But no one would listen to him. Because Lowndes County had to get somebody, and it had to be a black man, to pay for the murder of Mr. Lane, they let all the white men go who could have been involved or who knew something about Mr. Lane's murder. I spoke to a white lady who was working there at the time, and until today I don't understand how the case was handled. This white source stated they never saw anything happen like this before in the court of law. I say to you, if you don't have a lot of money to hire a good lawyer, the same thing could happen to you. That's why so many blacks are in jail now for crimes they did not commit and many will never be free. Once they get out of jail they are placed on probation, and as soon as they find themselves in the wrong place, they are sent back to jail. That's what happened to my brother, Ollie. He was at the wrong place at the wrong time.

After they arrested Ollie, they stopped looking for the real person who killed Mr. Lane. Oh! And remember now Ollie was only seventeen years of age. So just think about a black man seventeen years old, walking in a white man's house, and finding him dead, with two white men there also. In the year of 1962, within the law, all eyes were on

Ollie. The Lowndes County Sheriff's Department and the G.B.I. didn't take time to find the one who really killed Mr. Lane. Ollie kept telling them over and over that he did not kill Mr. Lane. Ollie told his Dad over and over again, "Dad, I did not Kill Mr. Lane." And I do believe if my brother had committed that crime he would have told our Dad the truth. I do believe he would have told his oldest brother, Johnnie Lee the day before he was executed. As Johnnie told me that he asked Ollie point blank, "Did you kill Mr. Lane?" And Ollie's answer was, "No, I did not kill Mr. Lane." So, if you know that you are going to die, you would tell the truth to your family, and ask God to forgive you. But in Ollie's letters he never mentioned one time about forgiveness. He would always say, "I did not kill Mr. Lane." He also said,

> "They made me say I took $60.00 from Mr.
> Lane's wallet. How did they know Mr. Lane
> had $60.00 in his wallet when his wallet was
> never found? And how did he shoot Mr. Lane
> with his gun when his gun was not working?
> It was an old gun that his dad had given him

and no one could find the part for that model gun. I kept telling them that I was innocent, but they kept beating me, so I just gave up and said what they told me to say."

So after they took his life, there was a white man on his deathbed, as he was getting ready to leave this world saying, "They killed that nigger for nothing." It was nothing we could do about it because by then they had already executed my brother. The white man who confessed had also died. To those of you who did not do your job, and wanted to see a black man die for something he did not do, I am going to leave this weight on your heart and let your conscience be your guide. I believe and I know you will pay for killing my brother, for a crime he did not commit, because I believe that Mr. Lane, whom you say Ollie killed, would not have wanted you to kill Ollie for something he did not do. I believe Mr. Lane liked Ollie. He liked the way he did his work and the way Ollie talked about Mr. Lane seemed like they both got along well. I do believe they were good friends.

That's why we all know that my Ollie did not murder Mr. Lane. Ollie cared a lot for Mr. Lane and Mr. Lane cared a lot for my Ollie. They got along good together. Someone out there did not like to see them together and decided to murder Mr. Lane and frame my Ollie for his murder. Oh how happy the Chandler family would be if the real murderer would confess to the murder of Mr. Lane. Somebody out there somewhere knows that Ollie Chandler did not murder Mr. Lane. We just keep hoping and praying that someone will come forward and tell the truth about the murder. He or she would feel better within their soul and say finally I did one thing right and feel good about it. The Chandler family could shed tears of happiness. Our brother, Ollie's name would be cleared. My Mom would have been so happy if her son's, name was cleared for the murder of Mr. Lane before she passed away. She shed so many tears until she got sick. She cried out for her son until she passed away. She would always say my son didn't have a chance to grow up and have a family of his own, and to be the young man God wanted him to be. He just didn't have a chance. I would not wish that on anybody. Just imagine if Ollie was your son. How would you feel? What would you do or say to save your son when you know your son did not commit murder. Think about it as you read this true story.

I lay awake many nights shedding many tears thinking and thinking if I were older, what could I have done or said to help save my brother's life. Could I have made a difference with the judge, jury and all who helped sentence him to the electric chair? Would they have taken the time to listen to what I had to say? Or would they have given me the chance to do what I could to save my brother's life. I know our parents did all they could to save my brother's life. So, I will never know what if, what if? Because I was not old enough to say what if I could have done this or that, I will never know if my help could have made a difference. But I hope by writing this book somehow it will make a difference in my life and in the life of others.

And as it is in the State of Georgia now racism is still going on in some of the smaller towns, including wrongdoing toward blacks by law enforcement even in 2004. In the new millennium, James Williams was beaten to death by the law enforcement in Lowndes County, and nothing has been done about that. That goes to show how our civil rights are still being violated. We are still being killed by the law enforcement, but only in a different way as many young men have died in the hands of the Police Department and Sheriff's Department in Valdosta, Lowndes County. As James Williams was beaten to death, they say his autopsy shows something else. But I refuse to believe that, as well. Other young men have died in the hands of the Lowndes County Sheriff's Department. And that goes to show that things have not changed since 1962. The Law Enforcement just does it in a different way.

Note following pages:

encephalopathy to cardiac dysrhythmia, due to cardiomegaly with left ventricular hypertrophy.

2-Willie Lee Gaye, (BLACK), age 39, died 23 October 1995: CAUSE OF DEATH: Chronic Ethanolism

3-***** James N. Starling, (WHITE), age 63, died 1 May 1996: CAUSE OF DEATH: Coronary atherosclerotic disease

4-Willie James Williams, (BLACK), age 49, died 2 September 1998: CAUSE OF DEATH: Subdural Hemotoma

5-Ronzie Sonny Graham, (BLACK), age 48, died 13 July 2000: CAUSE OF DEATH: Uknown

6-Rosemary King, (NOT PROVIDED), Age 40, died 20 July 2001: CAUSE OF DEATH: High Blood Presure Hyper Tension

7-***** Richard William Oakley, (WHITE), age 27, died April 2002: CAUSE OF DEATH: Suicide/Hanging

8-Sandra J. Wallace, (BLACK), age 39, died 31 August 2002: CAUSE OF DEATH: Complications of Acquired Immune Deficiency Syndrome

9-Lisa Sanders, (BLACK), age 38, died 2003: CAUSE OF DEATH: Natural Cause

10-John Henry Dejonghe, (WHITE), age 49, died 21 June 2004: CAUSE OF DEATH: Seizure disorder in a background of chronic ethanolism

11-****** Amaruy Quinones, (HISPANIC), age 34, died 2 September 2005: CAUSE OF DEATH: Self Induced Staravation

12-Esavious Wright, (BLACK), age 29, died, 16 February 2006: CAUSE OF DEATH: Heart Attack

13-***** Bobby Stanford, (BLACK), age 55, died 23 March 2006: CAUSE OF DEATH: Aneurysm of Aorta

14-Clarence Fender, (WHITE), age 70, died 2 April 2006: CAUSE OF DEATH: Heart Attack

accident. Minister of truth, retired from the United States A Force, owned a sm business for fourte years, community organizer, Presider of local NAACP, member of Operati PUSH, Peoples Tribunal, member of the masonic lodge, published in many newspapers includi USA Today, maintained a radio broadcast in Conwa South Carolina (WLAT), while stat at Myrtle Beach Air Force Base, WGOV for two years with the Historical Gosp Giant Herman Smil Sr. Then on WJEM with the C.W.O. D. Broadcast (Community Words Deliverance). He w on radio eighteen years speaking tru to power, he NOW resides in Valdosta Georgia. To better know him READ HI BLOG. Because wh truth comes falsehood must VANISH and falsehood is foreve vanishing thing!

15. George Hill Jr., age 21, (BLACK), died 23 June 2006: CAUSE OF DEATH: Heart Attack

16.NAME OMITTED, but available upon request) (Black Female), SUICIDE, YEARS EARLIER. Following the State of Georgia NAACP, Press Conference at the Lowndes County Jail on July 5, 2006 at 1:00pm by President Edward DuBose.

Three family members and an associate of the family made another death known. This deceased inmate name is WITHHELD out of respect to the family. However, it is public record and has been verified.
What inmates said on May 5, 2005, is quickly becoming a reality. That more deaths had occurred in or surrounding the jail but not reported to the general public.

MOREOVER, it may be a good idea to check with the local News Media and verify the dates, and within what time frame these deaths identified by an (*) were reported to the public by the local media. And if there were more deaths. Why were they not reported to the general public in a timely manner?

Above identified American Citizens (Inmates) came from the Valdosta Daily Times, Lake Park Post, calls from jailed inmates, public records, and from the Sheriffs Department own records given to Edward DuBose of the NAACP for the State of Georgia following his press conference held at the Valdosta-Lowndes County Jai

AGAIN! Inmages say there have been more but not reported to the public! (May 5, 2005) Names available upon request....

Also GOOGLE, A VIDEO "A CHORUS OF FEAR AND WILLIE JAMES WILLIAMS DEATH IN LOWNDES COUNTY JAIL"

*IF YOU KNOW OF OTHERS! PLEASE INFORM THE NAACP STATE OF GEORGIA OFFICE SO THEY CAN UPDATE THEIR DADA BASE FOR ALL DEATHS WHILE IN THE CUSTODY OF LAW

For Ollie, blood still cries out from the grave for justice. But as I grew up and got older, I tried to find justice for my brother, Ollie. I went to my Dad and told him what I was going to do, but my Dad and my Mom was still afraid for themselves and the children because they loved their children so much. After a long time my mother would still break down in tears because she loved her son so much, much like any mother not wanting her child killed under any circumstances, for something he did not do. For Ollie's blood still cries out from the grave for justice.

As for me, I don't hate anybody, black or white, because I know that all of you that were involved in this case including those from the Judges chambers and the jury box, your sin will testify for you. Then God will punish you for your wrongdoing. Our father worked on one of the best paying jobs during that time, and had for 27 years. After this they were told not to hire any of the Chandler family. A lot of other companies were told the same thing because of the murder of Mr. Lane. They were led to believe that our brother committed the crime. So you see my family suffered as well because they accused Ollie for the murder of Mr. Lane. We all know that he was innocent. So you see there was a lot of hardship in our family.

In closing, you see when you are accused of something you did not do, a lot of pain, suffering, and tears follow, and worst of all, sometimes death. So I hope and pray that no one else will have to go through what our family went through in life. Things have gotten better now, and hopefully we won't have to suffer, as before, for a crime our brother did not commit.

Chapter 9

Postlude

His blood cries out from the grave for justice. This book is about my remembrances of the Chandler family during the years of 1962. There were so many more tragedies in our family. Ollie was not the only tragedy, but he was the one who paid with his life. There was a man killed, who was not a family member, but this killing set in motion a chain of events that has yet to be resolved. That man, for whom my brother worked for many years, was the main character, other than Ollie, about whom I have written. The man was killed by persons unknown, and they have seemingly gotten away with murder.

In reflection, and to restate what has already been stated, my brother, Ollie, was in the field doing the work that he had been hired to do. He heard a shot, and went to his employer's house to see what was going on. Upon his arrival, there were two men in the house – and because Ollie was fearful of what the men would do to him, he did exactly what he was told to do. His fingerprints were on everything – including Mr. Lane's wallet. These men also made sure that Mr. Lane's blood was on Ollie's clothing. Ollie, even though he was mentally challenged, knew that as a Black man, his word would not stand against a white person.

I still contend that my brother was framed. The police, the prosecutor, the judge, the witnesses, the jury and all of those who were involved in this case were all instrumental in perpetuating the cover-up. I do believe that all of these people must stand before the final Judge – and the books will be opened. The case will be recorded, and the truth will eventually come out. When the charges are read before the Judge, I believe that my brother will get the justice that he deserves. My brother's blood is crying out for that justice.

Justice for being held in the Lowndes County jail until he turned 18 years old and could be tried as an adult; justice for being framed for a murder that he did not commit; justice for the agony that his family suffered as they saw their loved one die a slow death each day that he was unjustly kept in a prison system that was corrupt; justice for the horrible death he suffered in the electric chair as he was burned to a crisp – and his flesh just crumbled away like dry cinders.

In the final analysis, as these guilty ones stand before the Judge, witnesses will not have to be called – for their deeds will testify against them. The guilty will stand before the Righteous Judge – and their sins will cry loudly. Just as my brother pleaded for mercy, those guilty will stand before the Judge pleading for mercy: not only for the death of my brother, but for the death of my mother – whose heart was broken and who could not stand the suffering any longer and breathed her last breath calling for her son. I still cry today for my brother, and what he might have been. I cry for the fact that he became the sacrificial lamb for a person or persons unknown. I cry for the injustice that was resident in a system that inferred that as long as someone pays for the crime, it doesn't matter whether they are guilty or not. For it was a well-known fact that a Black man's life was not nearly that of a White. A Black man was only 1/5th of a person – and therefore, could not think or feel or even be worthy of living his life. A guilty White man was far more worthy of life than an innocent Black!

I reflect on the times that our family had together as we were growing up – the fun we had, as we would work together, play together, sing songs, doing things that families normally do. I reflect on that day when my brother was snatched away from that loving family and placed into a situation from which there was no escape. I can still hear my dad telling us that Ollie was not guilty – that he was just trying to save his own life because he knew that those men in the house would kill him. But if they had killed him, whom would they have blamed for Mr. Lane's death? Who would have become the sacrificial lamb? No, Ollie was necessary in order for their scheme to work. He was expendable – he was a nobody – and he could be the one upon whom the sin was placed. He could be the scapegoat, the one not guilty of the act of murder, but guilty of being Black in a white south.

I cry for my family and what we could have been had our lives not been consumed by this tragedy, with trying to get justice for our brother. I cry for my father who, after so long, could not stand the pressures which were brought to bear on him and my mother, and who had to turn and get out for his own sanity. I cry for all of those who have suffered like fates – and who are yet crying out for justice.

I cry for the fact that my father and the family members were not able to get decent work because the companies were told not to hire any of the Chandler family. I cry for what may have been – and what was not. I cry for the missed opportunities and the harsh realities. I cry for the life of fear that my parents and family lived – in the south during that brutal time.

I cry for the man who, laying on his deathbed years later after this travesty of justice, knew of Ollie's innocence, and claimed that Ollie was killed for nothing. The man who said that there was nothing that he could do about it because Ollie was already dead. I cry for the guilt that this man endured for the years prior to his own death. I cry for his shame in not clearing Ollie's name when he had the chance. His guilt lies in the fact that he knew of Ollie's innocence, but failed to acknowledge it.

Dear reader, don't think that this has been related as a result of hatred – it hasn't! I don't have the energy to hate – and I don't want my life to be ruined because of hatred of those who do not deserve even hatred. For in order to hate, I must feel – and for those who were involved in this miscarriage of justice, I do not feel. I am empty and void of any feelings for them. My purging is complete – and the emptiness that I now feel is a relief. The burden of the negative emotions that were buried deeply within for so long – emotions which needed to be released – has been lifted. Why did I carry it for so long? Why did I allow myself to be yoked to a comrade who thought only to take my life, as Ollie's was taken? My death would only have been further proof that the guilty were still in control – and they have controlled long enough. There have been too many casualties – and it had to end. My hatred of those evil men would have continued to perpetuate the injustices of a system that was corrupt. I have been victim long enough – and I call heaven and earth to record this day the fact that I have been set free and I am no longer bound.

The insidious growth that began within the deepest recesses of my soul and which stayed with me for over 40 years – growing and consuming me on a daily basis, has been excised. I had to be willing to bear the pain of having the growth removed. I have faced the giant, and he has been conquered. I have overcome that which had been overcoming. My healing has begun – and just as the Man of LaMancha, I dreamed what I thought was an impossible dream, but that dream is now a reality - I beat the unbeatable foe.

> *"Dearly beloved, avenge not yourselves, but rather give place unto wrath: for it is written, Vengeance is mine; I will repay, saith the Lord."*

"HIS BLOOD CRIES OUT"

"And He said, What hast thou done? The voice of thy brother's
blood crieth unto me from the ground.
(Genesis 4:10)

Walter Chandler
© January, 2006
Draft I

Notes

Notes

Notes

Notes

Notes

Notes

Notes

Notes

Notes

....

....

....

....

....

....

....

....

....

....

....

Notes